Oats and Wild Apples

Frank Asch

Holiday House / New York

Library of Congress Cataloging-in-Publication Data

Asch, Frank.
Oats and wild apples.

SUMMARY: A calf and fawn meet and learn about
each others' lives, but in the end prefer to be
near their mothers.
[1. Mother and child—Fiction.   2. Cows—Fiction.
3. Deer—Fiction]   I. Title.
PZ7.A7780at 1988   [E]   87-17742
ISBN 0-8234-0677-6

For my mother

One day Calf asked Mother Cow to play.
"Want to run and jump with me?"
Mother Cow looked up from chewing her cud.
"Sorry, but I'm not in the M–O–O–D."

So Calf decided to play on her own.
Running through the pasture, she kicked up her heels,
jumped into the air and fell flat on her face!

"Hee, hee, hee!" Calf heard laughing.
  She stood up and walked over to the fence.
"Who laughed at me?"

"I did," said Fawn, and stepping out of the shadows,
  he jumped over the fence.
"Wow! What a terrific jump!" exclaimed Calf.

"Oh, that was nothing," said Fawn, nibbling some
grass from the pasture. "MMM, tasty, but I like
wild apples better. Want to come chase butterflies?"
"Sure," said Calf. "I see one over there."
And they both ran after it. As soon as they got
close, the butterfly fluttered up into the sky.
Round and round the pasture they frolicked until . . .

. . . the butterfly flew through the fence.

"Come on," cried Fawn. "It's getting away."

Calf hesitated. What would Mama think?
Then, crouching down, she squeezed under
the fence and followed Fawn into the forest.

Fawn was waiting by the brook.
"You took too long. It got away. But watch this,"
he said and nudged a frog with his nose.
The frog hopped and landed in the water with a splash.
"That looks like fun!" exclaimed Calf. "Can I try?"
Now Calf and Fawn had a new game, *Frog Nudging*.

After a while, Calf said, "I'd better be going
home now. Mama will be worried."
"Oh, don't go!" cried Fawn. "Come with me,
and I'll show you where the wild apples grow."
Calf had never tasted wild apples before.
"Okay," she said, "but then I really have to go."

"Follow me," said Fawn, and he led Calf deeper and
  deeper into the forest.
"Where's *your* mama?" asked Calf as they walked
  beneath the tall pines.
"I don't know," said Fawn. "We got separated last
  night when the wolves were chasing us."
"Wolves!" exclaimed Calf. "That sounds terrible."
"Only if they catch you," replied Fawn.

"But aren't you worried that you'll never see your
mama again?" asked Calf.
Fawn didn't answer. For a long while they traveled
silently through the forest. Fawn was thinking
about his mama and Calf was thinking about hers.
She was also thinking about wolves.
"Maybe," she pondered, "wild apples aren't
so important after all."

Calf was about to ask Fawn to lead her back to the
pasture when they came upon a clearing.
In the center of the clearing was a large wild apple tree.
Bounding toward the tree, Fawn reached up and pulled
down a branch so Calf could grab one of the wild apples.
"Now, isn't that better than the grass from your pasture?"
asked Fawn.
"Almost better than the taste of oats," replied Calf.

"Oats?" puzzled Fawn, taking an apple for himself.
"What are oats?"
"The farmer gives them to us in the barn," said Calf.
"They taste very good."
  Calf and Fawn ate many apples that afternoon, as many
  as they could reach. Then Calf asked to go home.
"I miss my mama," she said.
  Fawn nodded and led the way back through the forest.

By the time they got to the pasture, the sun was
going down and the pasture was empty.
"Mama!" cried Calf. "Mama's gone! I want my mama!"
"Take it easy," said Fawn. "She's got to be here somewhere . . .
unless maybe . . . the wolves . . ."
"Oh, no!" moaned Calf. "The wolves got her!"
And she began to shake with fear.

But suddenly she stopped. "Silly me. The farmer . . . of course!
He must have taken her back to the barn."
"The barn?" said Fawn.
"That's right," said Calf. "It's that way, behind those trees."
Now Calf led the way. Smelling the strange smells of
the barnyard, Fawn followed Calf past the farmer's house and
the chicken coop, into the dark shadows of the barn.

Calf knew exactly where to go to find her mother.
    Rushing up to her side, she called out "Mama!"
"Where have you been, child!" exclaimed Mother Cow.
"I was so worried, I was afraid my M–M–MILK would turn sour."

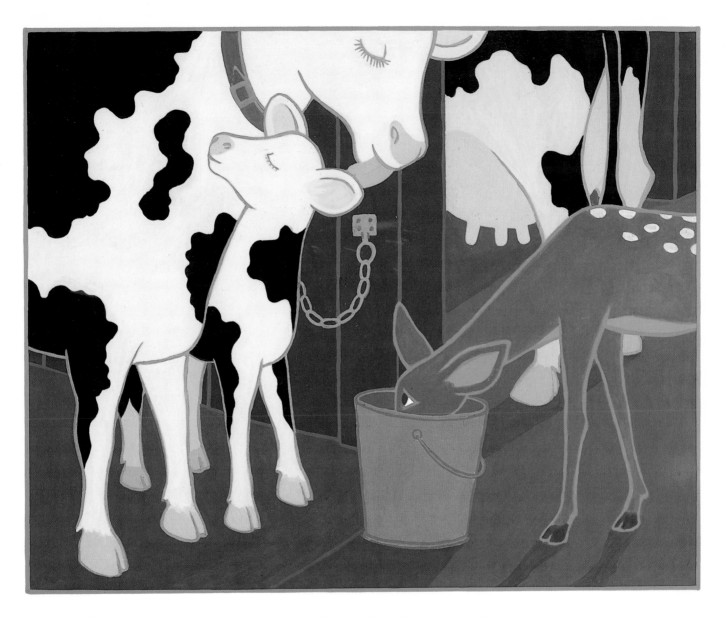

"Mama, this is my new friend. May we share some
of our oats with him?"
"Help yourself," said Mother Cow to Fawn.
"Thank you," replied Fawn, and he ate some of the oats.

"Don't they taste good?" asked Calf.

"Very good," replied Fawn.

Calf thought for a moment.

"Maybe you can stay and live with us. I bet you'd like it here.
In fact, I know you would! Oh, please say you'll stay."
Fawn was just about to answer when a shadow
appeared at the door.

When Fawn saw who it was, his heart leapt with joy.
"It's my mama!" he cried.
Calf watched while Mother Deer greeted Fawn
with an affectionate lick.

"Thanks for the oats!" called Fawn.
"You're welcome," replied Calf.
"Thanks for the wild apples."
 And she watched while Fawn and Mother Deer
bounded into the night.